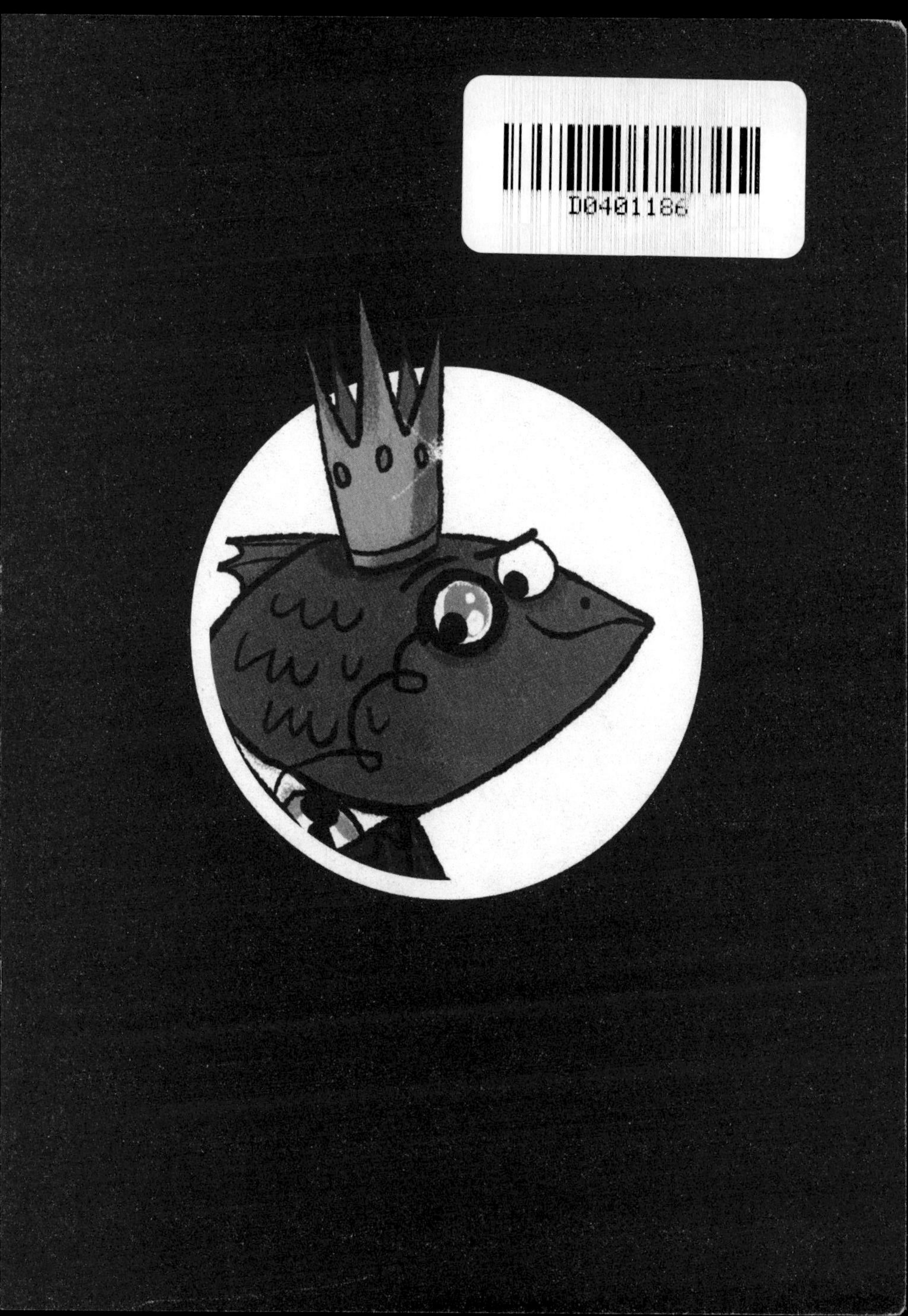
D0401186

RIDER WOOFSON

SOMETHING SMELLS FISHY

BY WALKER STYLES • ILLUSTRATED BY BEN WHITEHOUSE

LITTLE SIMON
New York London Toronto Sydney New Delhi

LITTLE SIMON
An imprint of Simon & Schuster Children's Publishing Division
1230 Avenue of the Americas, New York, New York 10020
First Little Simon paperback edition January 2016

Also available in a Little Simon hardcover edition.

For information about special discounts for bulk purchases, please contact Simon & Schuster Special Sales at 1-866-506-1949 or business@simonandschuster.com. The Simon & Schuster Speakers Bureau can bring authors to your live event. For more information or to book an event contact the Simon & Schuster Speakers Bureau at 1-866-248-3049 or visit our website at www.simonspeakers.com. Designed by Laura Roode.
The text of this book was set in ITC American Typewriter.
Manufactured in the United States of America 0816 MTN
2 4 6 8 10 9 7 5 3
Library of Congress Cataloging-in-Publication Data
Styles, Walker. Something smells fishy / by Walker Styles ; illustrated by Ben Whitehouse. — First Little Simon paperback edition. pages cm. — (Rider Woofson ; 2) Summary: "Prince Bubbles, the prince of New Sealand, comes to Pawston to receive an award. Everything goes swimmingly well until Rider and the P.I. Pack realize something smells fishy about their royal visitor"— Provided by publisher. ISBN 978-1-4814-5741-5 (pbk) — ISBN 978-1-4814-5742-2 (hc) — ISBN 978-1-4814-5743-9 (eBook) [1. Mystery and detective stories. 2. Detectives—Fiction. 3. Dogs—Fiction. 4. Animals—Fiction. 5. Impersonation—Fiction. 6. Princes—Fiction.] I. Whitehouse, Ben, illustrator. II. Title.
PZ7.1.S82So 2016
[Fic]—dc23
2015018118

CONTENTS

chapter
ONE

A Prince in Pawston

"What in Pawston is going on?" Rider Woofson barked. The dog detective was driving his P.I. (Pup Investigators) Pack to their favorite diner to celebrate solving their latest case. But cars were bumper to bumper, and the traffic wasn't moving. Rider didn't like sitting still, not when he could be solving a super-crime.

"Maybe I can see what's happening with my new Seeing Eye Dog Glasses," Westie Barker said as he wagged his tail excitedly. This white terrier was a detective *and* an inventor, and he loved trying out his new gadgets. Westie adjusted his homemade invention that was raised over the traffic. "It's a real zoo at the Pawston Marina. Half the city must be there . . . and everyone has cameras. Wonder what all the hubbub is about."

"The marina?" Rora Gooddog looked up from her book. "Is it Tuesday already? I almost forgot about Prince Bubbles."

"Who's Prince Bubbles?" Westie asked.

“If he’s not a super sub sandwich with mayo and extra marshmallows, who cares? I’m hungry!” Ziggy whined. He was the youngest of the P.I. Pack, and he always thought with his stomach.

"Prince Bubbles is fish royalty," Rora answered, "from the under-water country of New Sealand."

"Hey, isn't that the prince who hardly ever leaves the water? I wonder what brings him to dry land," Rider said, parking the P.I. van. "I'd like to go investigate. You've caught my curiosity."

"You know what they say," Ziggy whined, rubbing his empty tummy. "Curiosity killed the cat."

"Good thing I'm no cat," Rider said as he fixed his hat.

At the Pawston Marina, a crowd of fans had gathered around the dock, which was covered with a fancy red carpet. There was a velvet rope, and several security guards were holding the fans back from a long blue limousine. Among the guards was a French bulldog who Rider recognized from a previous case. "Heya, Frenchie," Rider said. "What are you doing here?"

"I'm working as security for the prince. He's here visitin' Pawston to be awarded the Key to the City for his clean water program. Pretty neat, huh?"

Before Rider and the P.I. Pack could ask more questions, the animals went wild. A plank emerged from the water and landed on the dock. A glittering, bedazzled fishbowl with giant wheels drove up the plank, moving slowly out of the water.

Inside the fishbowl, there was a single castle. The crowd became

very quiet. "Where's the prince?" everyone whispered.

Suddenly, Prince Bubbles swam through the castle doors and emerged at the top of the fish-bowl, waving his fins. The crowd shouted with glee.

"That's what I call regal, kid," Rora said to Ziggy.

"Well, I'm royally hungry," Ziggy said. He followed his nose into the crowd, sniffing around for a snack.

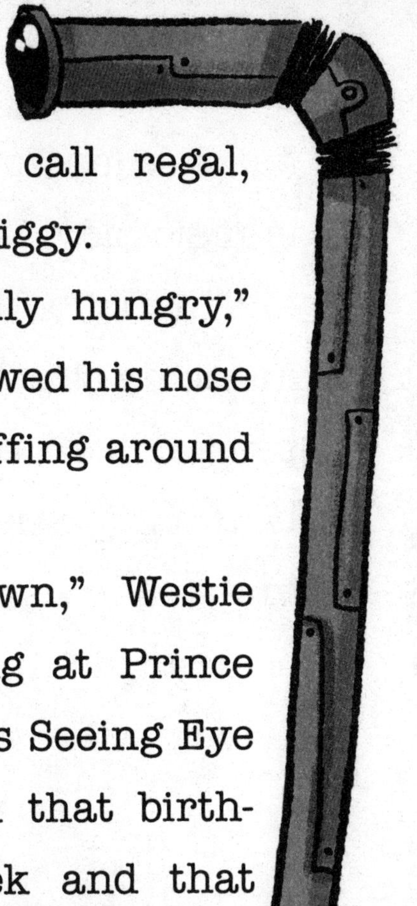

"I like his crown," Westie noted while looking at Prince Bubbles through his Seeing Eye Dog Glasses. "With that birth-mark on his cheek and that monocle on his eye, he certainly is majestic."

The fishbowl drove to the limo. Frenchie closed the door after the prince disappeared inside.

Having failed to find a snack in a trash can, Ziggy popped his head up just in time to see the limo driver, who was scratching his

mustache. He looked familiar—but why? Could Ziggy have known that rottweiler? Before the pup could place him, the rottweiler winked at Ziggy, and the limo sped away. Prince Bubbles was gone.

chapter
TWO

The next day, the P.I. Pack was back in the office. Rider was reading old case files. Rora was flipping through the newspaper. Westie was fiddling with his latest invention. Bored and a little hungry, Ziggy turned on the TV.

"Hey look! Isn't that the prince?" Westie said, pointing to the TV.

Prince Bubbles was on the news, shaking hands with the mayor and the police chief. "It was *paw-some* seeing him in person yesterday, huh?"

"Well, that prince sure swims around town," Rora noted. She held up a newspaper article about

the prince reading stories to children at a public school.

"Bubbles-mania has taken over Pawston . . . tonight on *Sea*lebrity News!" said a parrot reporter on the TV. "Last night, Prince Bubbles was seen going to dinner at Pawston's hottest new underwater

restaurant, KELP! And who was his date? Why, the beautiful and electrifying Ellie Eel."

Ziggy stopped flipping channels. Instead, he hopped up onto the desk and sniffed at the images of Prince Bubbles on the TV screen.

"What's up, pup?" Rora asked. "You thinking about eating the TV?"

"No. There's something weird about that prince," Ziggy said. "I can't quite put my paw on it."

"Always trust your instinct, Zig," Rider said. "Instinct is a dog's best friend."

Suddenly the buzzer rang. Rora got up to answer the door. "Oh boy! We have company!" Westie said, his tail wagging. "I wonder if they'd be interested in helping me test my latest invention: the Grip-o-matic Grabber."

"Keep the science to yourself,

partner," Rora said. "Our visitor looks seasick and in need of help."

The fish wore a full-body scuba suit and a fishbowl on his head. He walked into the room and smiled. "Hello. Is this the P.I. Pack Detective Agency?"

"It is. Can I get you some water?" Rider asked kindly. He slid a chair over to the rather nervous-looking fish.

"Oh my, yes," the fish said. "I'm as dry as turkey jerky." As the fish sat down to catch his breath, he seemed a little better, but still

a little nervous. Westie went for water as the P.I. Pack crowded around their visitor to listen to his story. "Thank you for having me. I didn't know where else to turn."

"Let's start at the beginning," Rider said. "What's your name?"

"Red. Red Herring."

"How can we help, Red?" Rora asked.

"Well, I have a mystery that needs to be solved, only I can't really prove it's a mystery in the first place, which is why I didn't know who else to talk to who won't think I'm crazy. Can you help?"

"You came to the right place," Rider said.

chapter
THREE

A FISHY TALE

Westie handed Red a glass of water. The fish looked at it and returned it immediately. "Sorry to trouble you, but could I have a glass of water with salt in it?" Red asked.

"Saltwater?" Ziggy moaned. "What kinda fish are you?"

"A herring of course," Red explained. "We live in the ocean

and are quite different from freshwater fish, naturally. I'm from New Sealand."

"Do you know Prince Bubbles?" Westie asked excitedly.

"Yes and no," Red said. "You see, I know the *real* Prince Bubbles. But the fish parading around Pawston . . ." Red pointed at the TV screen, where the news reporter was interviewing the prince. "He's an impostor!"

"Did you say *pasta*?" Ziggy yelped, his ears perking up.

"No, I said impostor!" Red repeated. "That is *not* my prince."

"How do you know?" Rider asked.

"Last night, I went to have dinner at KELP. The prince was there, and when I said hello, he pretended to be on his *shell*phone. Like he didn't even know me! He didn't shake my fin or stop to wave, even! Can you imagine?"

"I certainly can, Red," Rora said. "If I were a royal, I wouldn't be running around touching paws with every goon and dame that looked my way."

"Then you have never visited New Sealand," Red said, offended. "In my country, we are all very kind—especially the royals. For the prince to not wave to a citizen—in fact, to not even recognize a citizen of his kingdom—is unheard

of. Prince Bubbles is a friend to every fish in the sea."

"Your story is walking on thin ice," Rora said, not convinced. "I'm not buying it. New Sealand is a large kingdom. I can't imagine Prince Bubbles knows *every* fish."

"But he does!" Red said. "He has the memory of an elephant fish."

"Give me a *break*, and *fast*," Rora huffed.

"Did someone say *breakfast*?" Ziggy asked. When everyone shook his or her head no, Ziggy's tummy growled. He was hungry.

"I am offended!" Red said. "I am being treated like a lying *slob*ster. I would never make up such a *whale* of a tale!"

"This guy's story is a hook, line, and *stinker*,"

Rora said. "It's a stretch at best."

"Now, Rora," Rider said, "let's hear the fish out."

While the others talked, Ziggy started sniffing around the office. He'd hidden his bone here somewhere, but he couldn't quite recall where. His nose led him past Rora's desk, where his wagging

tail hit her newspaper and it fell to the floor. Ziggy couldn't believe his eyes. "Well, I'll be a puppy's uncle."

Ziggy picked up the newspaper and brought it over to his friends. "*Bow-wowza!* Red is telling the truth!" Ziggy exclaimed. "And I can totally prove it!"

chapter FOUR

THE MAYOR'S OFFICE

Ziggy laid out Rora's newspaper. "See anything weird?" he asked the others.

"Good job, Ziggy," Rider said, patting the pup detective on his head.

"I don't see anything," Westie said, staring at the two images of Prince Bubbles. The first was

an old photo of the prince on his throne in New Sealand. The second photo was taken here in Pawston just yesterday. Westie scratched his head with his Grip-o-matic Grabber. "I don't get it."

Rora smiled and said, "Whoever is impersonating the prince doesn't have a dog's eye for detail. Prince Bubbles's monocle and birthmark are reversed in these pictures."

"Clever dogs," Red said. "Now will you take my case?"

"We're already on it," Rider said, pulling his keys from his pocket. "Let's roll, P.I. Pack."

Minutes later, Rider and his crew marched into the

mayor's office, even though the mayor was in a meeting with Mr. Meow. Ziggy was about to show the mayor his newspaper finding when Rider grabbed it and put it in his back pocket. Rider winked, letting his team know to follow his lead.

"It'*ssss* e*ssss*pecially rude to

walk in on a meeting uninvited," Mr. Meow hissed.

"Mr. Meow, Mr. Mayor, I am sorry for the interruption," Rider said. "But the team and I were hoping for a treat. We would love to meet the prince while he's in town."

"He'*ssss* bu*ssss*y," Mr. Meow

said, looking at his claws. "He'*ssss* a prince, after all."

"I understand," Rider said politely. "But as a pup who grew up next to the City Kitty River, I know first-hand how important clean water is, and I'd like to thank the prince for his help."

"Mr. Meow is right," the mayor said. "The prince is quite busy. But I'd be happy to give you tick-ets to our Key to the City event. You might not get to meet him, but you'll be close to the action."

"I find it is best to be near the action," Rider said, eyeing Mr. Meow. He wasn't sure why, but the cat didn't seem to like him very much.

The mayor pulled out four tickets to the event. "Thank you, Mr. Mayor," Westie said. "I'll take those." Using his new Grip-o-matic Grabber, Westie

reached out. But the powerful invention shot past the tickets and knocked into some filing cabinets. The mechanical grabber was so strong, it pushed the filing cabinet over, which knocked over the next one, which knocked over the next one, and on and on. Like dominoes, all the cabinets fell on their

sides, throwing papers everywhere. “Sorry,” Westie said. “Let me try again.”

“NO!” everyone shouted.

“Thank you,” Rider said, quickly taking the tickets from the mayor. “We’ll see you there . . . and we promise not to make a mess of anything else.”

chapter FIVE

CLUES AND PLANS

As they left the mayor's office, Rora and Ziggy were upset. They were about to voice those feelings when Rider put his finger to his lips. "*Hush, puppies,*" he whispered. "Save the questions for when we're in the *bark*ing lot,"

As soon as they got in the van, Rora asked, "Rider, why didn't you tell the mayor that the prince is an impostor?"

"Because something smells *fishy*," Rider answered. "*Why* would someone impersonate the prince? If we answer that question, then we may stop a real crime before it happens. And the fewer people that know the prince is an impostor right now, the better."

"This is just like that case in New Yorkie," Rora said. "We have two missions: Number one, find out who has the prince. And number two, find out why."

"What's this?" Westie said to himself as he pulled a piece of paper off the end of his Grip-o-matic Grabber. "Eureka!" he yelped. "I have a theory about mission number two. This is from the mayor's office. It's the designs for the Key to the City."

"What's so important about the Key?" Rora barked.

"There is a smaller key inside the big key. And it opens up every door in Pawston!" exclaimed Westie. "Restaurants, stores, vet offices, museums, even bank vaults. You name it, this key can open it."

"Cocker-poodle-doo!" Ziggy said. "Any criminal would love to get their paws on that!"

"Westie, you're like a calculator," Rider said with a smile. "We can always *count* on you."

"Thank you, sir," Westie said. "But you should thank my Grip-o-matic Grabber."

"Looks like my hunch was right," Rider said. "It's a good thing we didn't alert the mayor. We have an impostor to find before he gets a free pass to open up every locked door in Pawston. And I know just the bait to use to hook him. Now, who feels like fishing for a bad guy?"

chapter
SIX
CEREMONY

THE OLD SWITCHEROO

The next day at the Key-giving ceremony, Rider and the P.I. Pack were in the front row. There was a red carpet leading to the stage, along with dozens of reporters and hundreds of fans ready to snap pictures of the royal fish.

When a limo arrived, the fans screamed with joy. But they were disappointed when the mayor stepped out with Mr. Meow and a glass suitcase. Inside the suitcase was a golden key—the Key to the City. The pair walked down the red carpet to the mayor's podium, carrying the glass case. "Here, let

me help," Rider volunteered.

"Thanks, Detective. It seems you're always around to lend a helping paw," the mayor said.

"More like you're always*ssss* in the way," Mr. Meow added under his breath.

"What was that?" Rider asked.

"Oh, nothing," the cat purred.

Rider carried the glass case to the podium. Once he set it down, he waved the rest of his P.I. Pack over. "We just wanted to thank you, Mr. Mayor," Rora said, shaking the mayor's hand.

Ziggy sniffed at Mr. Meow. "You smell salty."

"Mind your nose, and

your manner*ssss*," the cat hissed.

Then the crowd went wild again, screaming and shouting with excitement as another limo arrived. This time, Prince Bubbles emerged, stealing everyone's attention. "The prince draws quite

a crowd," Rider commented to the mayor.

"He sure does," the mayor said. "Isn't it wonderful?"

"It is practically *hiss*-torical," said Mr. Meow.

"Look at that entourage," Rora noted. The prince wasn't alone. By his side was his friend Ellie Eel. The famous pair was escorted by bodyguards—an octopus and a shark. They were all wearing the

latest above-water fashions that helped them breathe. Standing behind them was the limo driver, a mean-looking rottweiler.

Ziggy poked Rider. "Is it just me or does that driver with a mustache look like Rotten Ruffhouse?"

"It certainly does," Rider said. "Looks like our case just went from smelling fishy to smelling rotten."

With the ceremony beginning, Rider and the P.I. Pack left the podium and returned to their seats. As soon as they were sitting,

Rider leaned over to Westie. "Did you make the switch?"

"I sure did! I felt like Agent Double-O-Dog, James Bone himself." Westie wagged his tail. "With all eyes on Prince Bubbles, I used my Grip-o-matic Grabber to snatch the glass suitcase, replaced the real Key to the City with a fake, and put it back before anyone was the wiser."

"Good job, Westie," Rider said. As he eyed the limo-driving rottweiler, he smiled. "It looks like we're in for the *catch* of the day."

chapter
SEVEN

FISH-NAPPED!

"It is with great pride that I grant the Key to Pawston City to Prince Bubbles," the mayor said, speaking before the whole crowd. He was about to give the prince—well, the *impostor* prince—the golden key. The mayor and Mr. Meow stood before the prince and his friend Ellie Eel with the glass case and

the golden key. Suddenly there was a *whumpa-whumpa-whumpa* sound from high above the marina. A red helicopter swooped in and interrupted the mayor's speech.

The crowd was very surprised. They pointed to the sky and started asking questions. "Up there!" "Who is that?" "It's not a bird or a plane. It's a flying fish?"

"That looks like Red Herring!" Westie said, squinting.

Then before anyone could react, a fishnet from the helicopter dropped on Prince Bubbles and lifted him into the sky. The helicopter flew away. “The prince!” “He’s been *fish*-napped!” “Somebody help!” the crowd shouted.

"Yup, it's Red Herring," Westie confirmed. "But what's he doing? I thought he was on our side!"

"That's a red herring for you," Rider said. "They always send you barking up the wrong tree!"

"Oh dear," said Ellie Eel to the mayor. "Someone should help the prince. In the meantime, *I'll* hold on to the Key for him." Ellie snatched the

glass case with the golden key and slithered quickly toward the limo with the rest of the prince's crew. The rottweiler limo driver closed the door once they were inside, and then he hopped into the driver's

seat. As he hit the gas, he ripped off his fake mustache and threw it out the window.

"I knew it!" Ziggy cried. "It was that up-to-no-good Rotten Ruffhouse!"

"Interesting turn of events," Rider said, rubbing his chin. "I can't say I'm surprised though. Thank goodness we were two steps ahead. Team, it's time to divide and conquer."

"Westie and Ziggy, you two are Team Fetch," Rora ordered. "You follow the impostor prince and that helicopter. They should lead you to the real prince. Rider and I are Team Dog Run. We're going to chase those thugs and make sure

they don't make any more trouble. Let's go, teams."

Ziggy and Westie jumped into the van and followed Red Herring's helicopter. Using his Seeing Eye Dog Glasses, Westie tracked the helicopter and gave directions to Ziggy. The young detective was having so much fun driving that he forgot he'd skipped lunch. At least until they drove past a pizza stand and his nose got a whiff. "Yummy, yum, yum! Do you think we have time for some drive-through?"

"Certainly not!" Westie barked. "After that fishy fake prince!"

Meanwhile, Rider and Rora ran over to the barking lot and hopped onto their P.I. Pack motorcycles. Seconds later, the detective duo were roaring down the street

after the limousine. “Let’s fry some fish!” Rora shouted.

chapter
EIGHT

A WILD FISH CHASE

Rora and Rider zipped in and out of traffic on their motorcycles as they chased the limousine. The long luxury car was being driven by the villain Rotten Ruffhouse, and inside were the impostor prince's friends. It was up to the detectives to catch them before they got away.

"Watch out!" Rora shouted to Rider. "Octopus ink!"

The octopus bodyguard had rolled down the windows on the limo and was using all eight arms to throw buckets of slippery ink onto the road.

"Got it," Rider said, carefully avoiding the slimy puddles. "He may be well-*armed*, but I'm excellent on a bike."

Rider drove up a ramp and flew through the air, landing beside the limo. "Pull over!" he shouted at the driving rottweiler. "It's time for those fish to pay for their crimes and balance the *scales* of justice."

Rotten shook his head and stepped on the gas. Rider sped up too. Then he pulled a doggie bag

of old takeout food from his jacket and tossed it into the limo's sunroof. The car instantly filled up with a horrible stench.

"What was that?" asked Rora.

"Some food that Ziggy asked me to hold on to," said Rider with a smile. "Two months ago."

The limo pulled over and the villains jumped out, coughing at the awful smell. But before Rider and Rora could catch up, the bad guys ran toward the marina.

Meanwhile, on another road, Ziggy and Westie were tailing the

helicopter in the sky. The helicopter swerved sharply to the right, but there was no turn in the road. "They spotted us," Westie said.

"I'm not letting those fishy scoundrels off the *hook* that easily," Ziggy said. He drove the van off the road and through a grass field, following the helicopter. "Do you have an invention that could get a helicopter out of the sky?"

"Of course!" Westie said, pulling out his Grip-o-matic Grabber. "My Grabber can reach things near—and far!" He aimed the Grabber out the window toward the helicopter and then pushed the button. The Grabber arm reached up, up, up, way into the air and nabbed the helicopter. "Got 'em!" he cried. "Hit the brakes!"

Ziggy slammed on the breaks. The van jerked to a stop and so

did the helicopter. With nowhere else to go, the helicopter landed safely on the ground. "Let's make like a fisherman and *catch* these bad boys!"

Ziggy and Westie raced to the helicopter, but Red Herring and the fake prince leaped out. Then they ran toward the Pawston Marina, just like the other bad guys that Rider and Rora had been chasing.

The P.I. Pack came together, as all four dogs chased the bad guys down a dock toward a big sign that read:

"Hmm . . . do you think we need a reservation?" Rora asked.

"The only reservation I need is the law," said Rider. "Now let's turn the tide on this mystery."

chapter
NINE

A FISH AND SHIPS PLACE

"They're getting away!" Ziggy cried, pointing into the river as the fishy scoundrels and the scuba-suited rottweiler swam into the restaurant called KELP. The rest of the P.I. Pack were putting on scuba suits of their own.

"Ziggy, you stay up here and phone the police," Rider said. "And make sure no one gets away. We're going to *doggy* paddle down there and catch those sea urchins."

Rider, Rora, and Westie dove in and swam down to the underwater restaurant. The place was closed, but the doors were unlocked. Slowly, they swam inside. There was no sign of the crooks. "They could be anywhere," Rider said. "Keep your eyes open."

The three detectives swam around the massive place. The dining hot spot was one big aquarium. There were brightly colored trees

in between tables, the floors were made of marbles and rocks, and the ceiling had lovely nets decorated with starfish. There were even four castles, a pirate ship, and a giant black piano hanging from the ceiling. "KELP is such a so-*fish*-ticated place," Rora said. "I hope we're not underdressed. Hey, what's that?" Rora noticed that all of the castles said KELP, except one. It said HELP. Rora swam over

and found the real Prince Bubbles inside the plastic castle. He had been trapped there this whole time! "Hey, boys, I found my true prince!" Rora shouted to her partners.

"And the crooks found us," said Westie, pointing to the octopus, the shark, and Red Herring. Beside them were Rotten Ruffhouse, Ellie Eel, and the impostor prince with the golden Key to the City.

"Why'd you kidnap the prince?" Rider asked.

"I did it for the money," Ellie Eel said.

"And the rest of them work for me," said the impostor prince. He pulled off his fake birthmark and monocle. "They call me the *Cod-father*!"

"And the Key to the City?" Rider asked.

"Rotten hired us to steal it for his mystery boss." The Codfather grinned. He snapped his fin and the thugs stepped closer, each pulling out a giant swordfish. It looked like a sharp ending was in store for the P.I. Pack. "Any last questions?"

"Just one," Rider said. "How do you catch dirty fish?"

"How?" asked the Codfather.

"With a big net!" Rider grabbed a sea star from the wall and threw it. The sharp star cut the net decorations loose, which drifted down, trapping Ellie Eel, Red Herring, and the bodyguards. Rotten grabbed the fake Key to the City and escaped by swimming out of a window.

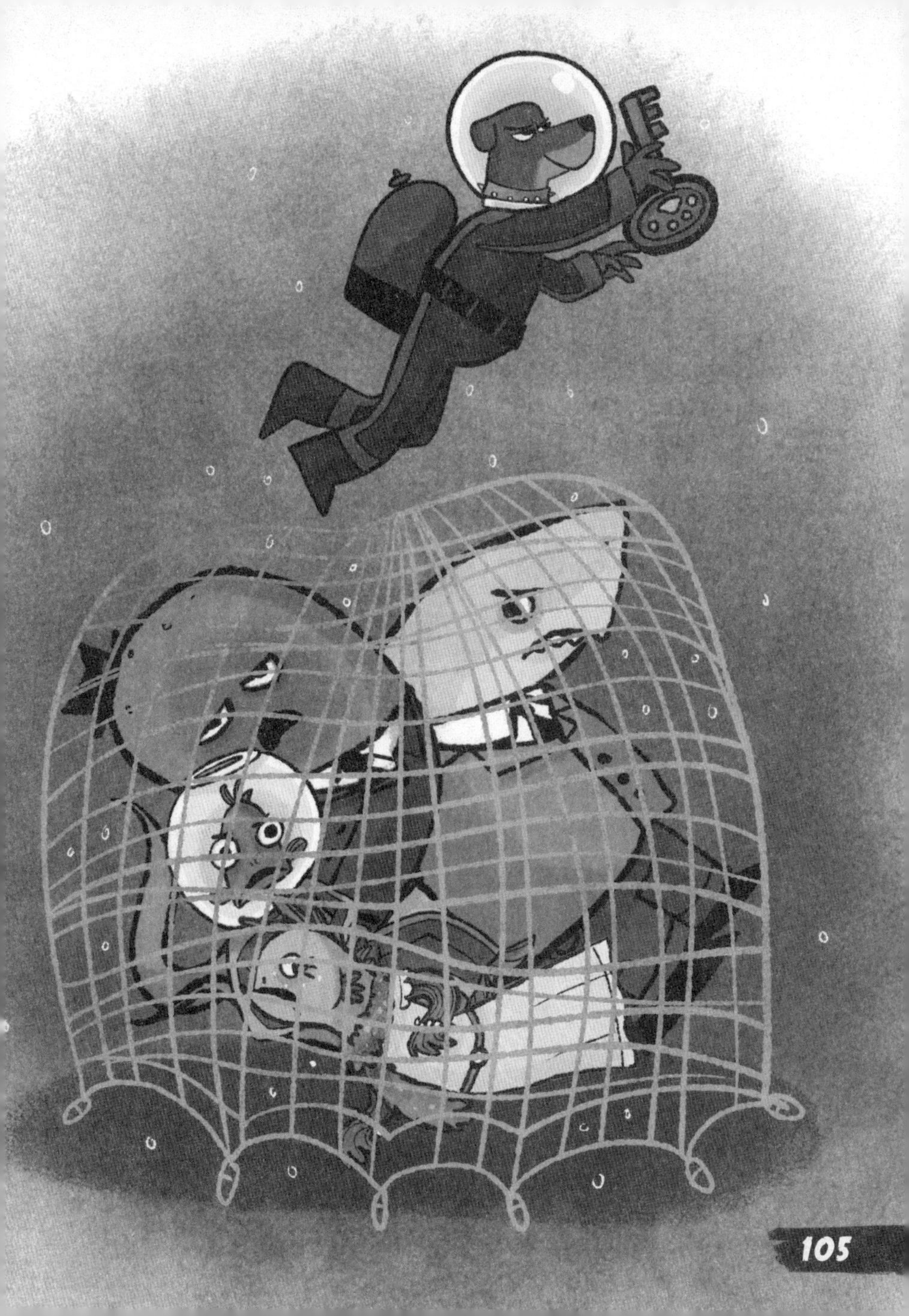

Rider was about to swim after him when the Codfather grabbed a swordfish the shark had dropped. "*En garde!*"

Rider found a swordfish as well,

and the underwater duel began.

Clink! Clank! Clink! Clank!

The dog detective and the Codfather parried and dodged each other's swordfish until Rider

backed the villain into a corner. Then with one *swipe*, he cut through a rope and the piano from the ceiling came crashing down on the bad guy.

"Do you know the difference between tuna and a piano?" Rider asked the moaning Codfather. "You can tune a piano, but you can't *tuna* fish."

"I'm not a tuna," the villain groaned. "I'm a cod."

"What you are," Rora said, handcuffing the cod, "is under arrest."

chapter
TEN

OFF TO SQUID ROW

The P.I. Pack swam out of the restaurant and climbed onto the dock. The *clam*bulances and police were waiting, and so was a very concerned mayor. The bad guys—all handcuffed together with coral reef—were escorted to the back of the police van.

"You saved the Key and the

prince!" the mayor said, flustered. "How did you do it, Rider?"

"All in a day's work," the detective said. "The bad guys were after the Key all along, and they knew the best way to get it was by impersonating the prince. They

tried to throw us off their scent by committing two crimes at once. While everyone was watching the prince being kidnapped, Ellie Eel made off with the Key to the City. Good thing my team had already used the same idea. We switched out the real key with a fake."

"I owe you my life," Prince Bubbles said to the detectives. "How can I ever repay you?"

"*Bow-wowza!* How about with an all-you-can-eat buffet!" Ziggy shouted excitedly. All that waiting outside of the restaurant had sure

made him hungry. "I'd be happy to eat whatever royal scraps you don't want. Cakes, ice cream, seaweed, whatever!"

"Please ignore my friend, Your Majesty," Rider said. "No payment is necessary. And I believe *this*

belongs to you." The dog detective handed the *real* key to the *real* prince.

"Wait a minute," Ziggy spoke up. "So where is the fake key?"

"With Rotten Ruffhouse and whoever he works for, which means they're in for a rude awakening." Rider smiled.

Across the city, Rotten ran down a set of secret stairs. "I have the key, Boss," he said.

Mr. Meow was waiting in his chair. "Fantasssstic," he mewed. "Finally, I have the Key to the City. It will open every door, and I can rob Pawston blind!" The sly cat took out a smaller key that was hidden inside the larger key and held it up.

"Does it really open every door?" the dog asked.

"Of courssssе," Mr. Meow said. "*Ssss*ee?" He pushed the key into his own door and turned it. Nothing happened. "It'ssss not working. Why isn't it working?"

Mr. Meow grabbed the larger Key to the City and rubbed his paw on it. Gold paint flaked off, and beneath it, instead of saying KEY TO PAWSTON CITY, it said KEY TO PAWSTON JAIL CELL #13.

"Confound that Rider Woofson!" Mr. Meow shouted with anger. "He pulled the old bait and *sssswitch* and gave me the key to the only door in the city that I do *not* want to open!"

CHECK OUT RIDER WOOFSON'S NEXT CASE!

Click-click-click-click. Crash! Clatter! Rat-a-tat! Boom!

"What's with all the noise?!" asked a floppy-haired mutt named Ziggy Fluffenscruff. "I was having the most amazing dream about a thirty-foot-long super-sandwich—until the noise woke me. Can't a pup take a *cat*nap in peace?"

Excerpt from *Undercover in the Bow-Wow Club*

"Sorry about that," said Westie. He was a brilliant West Highland terrier, and the P.I. Pack's inventor. "My latest creation can cause quite a commotion. I call it the Air-Drummer. It's half drum set, half ATV."

"I love TV!" Ziggy exclaimed, wagging his tail.

"Not a TV, kid," Rora Gooddog said, walking into the room. She was a poodle who was both smart and beautiful. "An *ATV*. It stands for 'All-Terrain Vehicle.' That means it can travel anywhere."

Excerpt from *Undercover in the Bow-Wow Club*

"Well, can it go get me something to eat?" Ziggy said, rubbing his growling belly. "I'm hungry."

"Not so fast, fella," Rora said to Ziggy. Then she turned to Westie. "Mind if I give it a try?"

"Of course!" Westie said, offering her the driver's seat. "It still has a few kinks to work out, but given the right driver—"

Rora started playing the drum set. *Rat-tat-tat a-ba-da ba-da-boom! Bada-da-da tada dada-da crash!*

"You're amazing!" Westie said.

Excerpt from *Undercover in the Bow-Wow Club*